This Walker book belongs to:

_____

_____

_____

First published 2016 by Walker Books Ltd
87 Vauxhall Walk, London SE11 5HJ

This edition published 2017

2 4 6 8 10 9 7 5 3 1

Original text © 1985–2005 Shirley Hughes Additional text © 2016 Shirley Hughes
Illustrations © 1985–2005 Shirley Hughes

The right of Shirley Hughes to be identified as author/illustrator of this work
has been asserted by her in accordance with the Copyright, Designs and Patents Act 1988

This book has been typeset in Plantin Light Educational

Printed in China

British Library Cataloguing in Publication Data:
a catalogue record for this book is available from the British Library

ISBN 978-1-4063-7381-3

www.walker.co.uk

MY FIRST
ABC

Shirley Hughes

WALKER BOOKS
AND SUBSIDIARIES
LONDON • BOSTON • SYDNEY • AUCKLAND

Aa is for aeroplane

High in the sky, an aeroplane zooms by.
Olly and I wonder how far away it is going.

Bb

is for bouncing ball!

When I throw my big shiny ball it bounces
away from me ... bounce, bounce, bounce.

Cc is for cat

Our cat is called Ginger. No cat is as nice as she is.

Dd

is for Dad who is very
good at cooking ...

and for our dog,
Buster, who always
wants to join in
with everything
we are doing.

Ee is for everyone

This is my family: Mum, Dad, Olly and me.

Ff

is for farm animals

There is a place in the park where we go
and see them up close.

Gg is for Grandma and Grandpa

They are very special. They often come to visit and look after us sometimes when Mum and Dad are busy.

H h is for hats

We have some great hats in our dressing up box.
Olly likes to try them on, even if they are too big
for him.

Ii is for ice cream

Grandpa always treats me to an ice cream
when we go to the park together.

Jj
is for jam and jar

When we've finished a jar of jam we can use
it for water to wash our paintbrushes and
keep our colours clean.

Kk is for Katie – that's me!

And this is my little brother Olly.

Ll is for leaves

In the autumn they turn
all kinds of beautiful
colours and you can
wade through them
when they fall from
the trees.

Mm is for Mum

I love having a cuddle with
Mum at the end of the day
when she reads my
bedtime story.

Nn is for noise

Olly and I can make lots of noise, especially when I am dancing and singing and he joins in with a saucepan and spoon.

Oo is for Olly, of course!

He can be annoying sometimes, but he loves it when we spend time together and we play some great games.

Pp

is for play-group

I have lots of fun at play-group with my
friends, jumping up and down on the
big cushions.

Qq is for queen

At Christmas, I got a crown in my cracker
and pretended to be a queen.

Rr is for rainbow

Sometimes, when it's sunny and rainy
at the same time, you can see a beautiful
arc of colours in the sky.

Ss is for stories

Olly and I love going to the library on Saturday
afternoons to listen to stories.

Tt is for toys

My favourite toy is called Bemily.
She is not quite a hippo and not quite a bear
and I take her with me wherever I go.

Uu is for umbrella

Olly and I have found a really good place to hide.

Vv

is for vacuum cleaner

It vroom-vroom-vrooms when Dad cleans the carpet.

Ww is for wellies

Olly and I need our wellies when we go out and splash in puddles.

 **Xx** is for kisses

Mum gave me an extra-special kiss when I gave her a birthday present all wrapped up in pretty paper.

 **Yy** is for yellow

Yellow is the colour of sunshine, and custard, and my favourite summery dress.

Zz is for zzzzz

Now it's sleepytime.

Good night, everyone!

Aa
apples

Bb
balloon

Cc
cat

Gg
goose

Hh
horse

Ii
ice cream

Mm
mug

Nn
nest

Oo
oranges

Ss
shoes

Tt
telephone

Uu
umbrella

Vv
vacuum

Dd
dog

Ee
egg

Ff
flowers

Jj
jug

Kk
kittens

Ll
leaves

Pp
pumpkins

Qq
queen

Rr
rabbit

Ww
watering can

Xx
box

Yy
yacht

Zz
zip